WHISPERS OF THE HEART

LIVIA XIA WANG

Made with ♥ on the Notion Press Platform
www.notionpress.com

Contents

Contents

Preface

Absolutely, it's disheartening to witness outdated perspectives on love and marriage persisting in our society. "Whispers Of The Heart" aims to challenge these notions and foster a more inclusive understanding of love. Regardless of whom we love, what truly matters is the depth of our affection, not superficial traits like gender, appearance, or financial status.

Marriage shouldn't be dictated by parents; it's a deeply personal decision. Parents' role should be one of acceptance and support, regardless of the gender. Nobody is flawless, and in the journey of marriage, both success and failure are inevitable. It's crucial for parents to stand by their children, offering unwavering support through all circumstances.

Embracing a broad-minded perspective is essential. Recognizing and accepting the realities of love in all its forms leads to a happier, more fulfilling life. Let's strive for a society where love knows no boundaries, where individuals are free to pursue happiness with whomever they choose, and where acceptance and support reign supreme.

Acknowledgements

I extend my heartfelt gratitude to those who walked alongside me on this literary journey. To my family, for their unwavering support and understanding during the countless hours devoted to crafting this tale. Special appreciation goes to my friends, whose encouragement and valuable insights enriched the narrative. My sincere thanks to the readers, whose curiosity and engagement breathe life into the words on these pages. Lastly, I express profound gratitude to the mentors and inspirations whose wisdom fueled my creative spirit. This story is a collective effort, and your presence in its creation is eternally acknowledged and cherished.

CHAPTER I

INTRODUCTION

Vikram Sharma, a trailblazer in the construction business for four decades, is a distinguished and noble figure. With a fair complexion, a half-bald head adorned with grey hairs, and an imposing height, he stands as a testament to the success born out of relentless determination. After getting married, he relocated to the southern part of India with the intention of initiating his own venture.

Starting his career from humble beginnings, Vikram overcame the challenges of his youth with unwavering perseverance, supported wholeheartedly by his wife. Acutely familiar with the hardships of poverty, he maintained a benevolent spirit toward his employees and engaged in charitable endeavours. Despite his success, Vikram upheld a strict demeanour with his children. His family, a testament to his enduring legacy, comprised his supportive wife, two sons, a daughter-in-law, and the joyous presence of two grandsons and a granddaughter.

Meera Sharma, the devoted wife of Vikram Sharma, stood steadfastly by his side through the highs and lows of their journey without a hint of complaint. Understanding intimately the challenges they had faced together, she emerged as a noble soul with a fair complexion, her grace accentuated by grey hair and an average height. Meera's unwavering support and resilience mirrored the shared experiences of overcoming life's bitter challenges. In her quiet strength, she became an integral part of Vikram's life, contributing to the foundation of their enduring bond and familial harmony.

Rakesh Sharma, a successor of the construction company, emerged as a sharp and astute business-minded individual. Displaying his acumen, he played a pivotal role in expanding their business operations to Singapore and Thailand. Settling in Singapore with his wife and two children, Rakesh, a tall and fair-complexioned man, exuded a determined demeanour.

Despite his success, he maintained a strict approach with his children, refraining from granting them much freedom. This discipline reflected his commitment to upholding standards and perhaps, his own experiences shaping a strong work ethic in the dynamic world of construction and business. He truly embodied the essence of an ironclad man.

Sheethal Sharma, the wife and business partner of Rakesh Sharma, epitomized a blend of fashion-forward sensibility and a bustling entrepreneurial spirit. As a busy woman immersed in the demands of their business, she found little time to spare for her children. Despite her hectic schedule, Sheethal remained a figure of discipline, consistently adhering to rules and imparting this ethos to her children. Her commitment to structure and order within the family reflected not only a dedication to their shared business ventures but also a desire to instil a sense of responsibility and adherence to principles in the next generation.

Yash Sharma, with his tall stature and fair complexion, harbours a silent turmoil beneath his composed demeanour. While his parents' strict rules confine him, he finds solace in the serene realms of literature and the expressive notes of the violin. Despite his outward appearance of compliance, Yash wrestles with inner frustrations, longing for autonomy and self-expression.

The handsome dimple adorning his left cheek hints at a hidden depth within him, a complexity veiled by his oval-shaped face. In the quiet moments of solitude, Yash delves into the pages of novels, finding refuge in the imaginative worlds crafted by words. The resonant melodies of his violin provide an outlet for his pent-up emotions, allowing him to express himself in ways his reserved nature cannot.

Amidst the rigid confines of his upbringing, Yash finds subtle liberation in the wisdom imparted by his grandmother and Uncle Rohith. Their gentle guidance offers a reprieve from the stringent expectations of his parents, allowing him to explore the nuances of his identity beyond conformity.

Despite his solitary disposition, Yash holds a deep admiration for his cousin Sidharth, the adopted son of his uncle. Sidharth's unwavering confidence and free-spirited nature serve as a source of inspiration for Yash, igniting a quiet yearning for independence and self-assurance.

Beneath the façade of compliance lies a burning ambition within Yash Sharma. Despite his reticence, he harbors dreams of carving his own path in the world as a successful architect cum entrepreneur. His aspirations, fueled by a desire for freedom and self-determination, drive him to seek avenues of creative expression beyond the confines of his childhood solitude.

Ankitha Sharma, with her vibrant spirit and passion for rap music and dance, embarked on a journey of self-discovery to find her artistic voice amidst societal expectations and self-doubt. Despite the challenges she faced, Ankitha's determination and resilience shone through as she navigated the complexities of pursuing her dreams. Alongside her brother Yash and cousin Sidharth, Ankitha found solace and support in their bond, each providing a unique perspective and encouragement along her journey. As she honed her skills and embraced her talents, Ankitha's character blossomed, revealing a dynamic and multifaceted individual who defied conventions and embraced her true passion with unwavering conviction.

Rohit Sharma, the younger son of Vikram Sharma, assumed responsibility for the family's business endeavors in Bharath. A noble figure with a fair complexion, Rohit mirrored his father's stature with a tall and commanding presence. Inheriting his father's philanthropic spirit, he actively engaged in charity works, displaying a compassionate approach toward both his employees and the community.

Despite his soft demeanour, Rohit, a keen businessman, demonstrated a firm hand in handling work-related matters, striking a delicate balance between empathy and professionalism. An unmarried man, Rohit dedicated himself to the success and welfare of the family business, perpetuating the values instilled by his father.

Sidharth Sharma, the adopted son of Rohit Sharma, shared his father's noble nature and gentle character. An obedient child, he cherished the stories narrated by his grandmother, forming a close bond with family traditions. Excelling in academics, Sidharth also revealed a majestic talent as a Carnatic singer, adding a melodious dimension to the family's cultural heritage.

Growing up, Sidharth discovered a profound passion for cooking, deriving immense joy from culinary pursuits. With a tall and commanding stature, he possessed a striking fair complexion that complemented his captivating cat eyes. His straight hair elegantly framed a heart-shaped face, creating the visual narrative of a young man whose diverse interests and talents intricately enriched the familial tapestry.

Sidharth harbours a dream of becoming a successful entrepreneur, aspiring to bring this vision to life through the establishment of a restaurant. Beyond his culinary endeavours, he is a jovial individual, consistently surrounded by a circle of friends who appreciate and share in his vibrant spirit. As he navigates the intricacies of his dual passions, Sidharth's character shines with authenticity and depth, making him a captivating figure in the familial saga.

Lena Franklin, the daughter of a family friend in the Rakesh Sharma circle, was born into affluence, living a life seemingly touched by a golden spoon. However, her demeanour left much to be desired, characterized by a presumptuous and arrogant attitude.

This behaviour did not sit well with Yash and Ankitha, the Sharma children, who found it challenging to warm up to Lena due to her off-putting nature. Despite the shared family connection, Lena's haughty disposition created a noticeable rift, making it difficult for genuine connections to blossom among the youngsters.

CHAPTER II

"Unexpected Symphony: A Journey Unveiled"

Yash Sharma reflects with a contemplative gaze, a peg of Vodka in hand, on the profound wisdom encapsulated in Napoleon Hill's words: "It is strange but true that the most important turning points of life often come at the most unexpected times and in the most unexpected ways." As he meticulously records his life's journey, he acknowledges that, indeed, his most pivotal moments unfolded in unforeseen ways. Among them stands a person who emerged as the transformative catalyst, weaving through the fabric of his narrative. With a sense of gratitude, Yash cherishes the unexpected encounter, recognizing it as a pivotal chapter in the story of his existence.

"I first encountered him as a baby when my uncle, Rohit Sharma, brought him home after his parents tragically perished in a car accident. Remarkably, he was in his mother's womb during the accident, and the medical team successfully saved him. Despite the lack of interest from his other relatives to adopt him, Uncle Rohit Sharma, deeply moved by the adorable infant, made a swift decision. Without hesitation, he chose to adopt the baby, ensuring a loving and caring home for the child.

However, my dad, Rakesh Sharma, and mom, Sheetal, initially disapproved of the adoption by Uncle Rohit Sharma. Within a year, we relocated to Singapore, and for a decade, we didn't return. It wasn't until my grandfather, Vikram Sharma, fell ill that we revisited with the family.

During this reunion, Sidharth's charming personality and mature demeanour had a profound impact on my parents. Despite being just ten years old, he engaged in conversations with a level of maturity that endeared him to my family, ultimately earning their admiration and approval.

He enjoyed playing with me, a four-year-old, and Ankitha, who was two years older than him. Both Ankitha and I grew fond of him. Whenever we faced scolding's from our parents, Sidharth was quick to comfort us with his amusing comic faces and drawings, reflecting his creative flair. His ability to bring joy to us through his imaginative expressions from his young mind, left a lasting impression. After two weeks, we returned to Singapore, promising our grandpa that we would visit again for vacations.

During the extended vacations at our ancestral home, we relished the complete freedom it provided. Uncle Rohit Sharma, recognizing his brother's strict approach, devoted ample time to be with us. He took us to the places we desired, prepared our favorited meals, engaged in play, and went the extra mile to ensure our happiness, particularly for Ankitha and me. Understanding the contrast between his brother's policies and our need for understanding, Uncle Rohit became a source of support. While my dad adhered to a policy where children were expected to unquestioningly follow his instructions, earning him the playful moniker "devil" from us, Yash fondly recalled these memories with a smile, reflecting on the bitter times of the past."

"Yashi, where have you been? I searched every nook and cranny of this house, calling out for you. Didn't you hear me?" Sidharth interrupted with concern while recording .

"Oh, you were looking for me. Today is truly the most beautiful day of my life. I was attempting to capture our story," Yash replied with a gleam in his eyes.

"Why would you want to do that today itself?" Sidharth asked, his emotions evident.

"I don't know, Sidhu. It just felt right, and you can share whatever you'd like about us," Yash expressed, a touch of sentiment in his voice.

"Alright, should we call it a day and pick up where we left off tomorrow? What do you think?" Sidharth inquired gently.

""As you wish, Sidhu. Oh, before we wrap up, let me formally introduce you. Meet Sidharth – the person I've been talking about. This marks the beginning of our story, the tale I yearn to share. So, good night," Yash conveyed with a twisted tongue.

"Oh, hi there! I'm Sidharth, eager to share more about our story. Look at Yash, happily lost in the moment. Let's connect again tomorrow," Sidharth exclaimed with joy, cradling the blissfully unconscious Yash in his arms.

Sidhu paused the recording, gently guiding Yash to the bed where he slept peacefully. Sidharth gazed at him with a tender smile, appreciating the beauty of the connection they shared, before taking his own turn to sleep.

In a moment filled with warm enthusiasm, Yash unfolded his vision to immortalize our story through a recorded video—a personal treasure for the future. He eagerly detailed his plan for a joint narration, where I, Shidhu, would interweave my thoughts whenever our schedules aligned. This collaborative approach promises a unique and heartfelt documentation of our shared journey.

As the day's conversation drew to a close, Sidharth took the initiative to cease the recording, marking the end of a chapter captured for their private nostalgia. The prospect of revisiting these shared moments through the lens of their individual narratives added a touch of intimacy to the project, ensuring that their story would be preserved in a manner that reflected both Yash's and Shidhu's distinct voices and experiences.

CHAPTER III

“Navigating Paths: Family, Work, and Well-being”

On Day two of recording, Sidharth’s captivating voiceover graced the session with a touch of beauty.

"Yash, affectionately known as Yashi at home, lived by a profound motto: “Define success on your own terms, achieve it by your own rules, and build a life you are proud to live.” This guiding principle encapsulated Yashi’s commitment to personal empowerment and authenticity. In embracing the mantra, Yashi sought a path uniquely tailored to individual aspirations, unbound by societal expectations. Through a dedication to self-defined success and adherence to personal rules, Yashi aimed to craft a life that resonated with a deep sense of pride.

Yashi, a Master in Architecture , found himself on a transformative journey shaped by his father’s vision. The paternal plan was clear – entrust the family company in Thailand to Yashi once he believed in his own capabilities. Shortly after his graduation, Yashi’s father facilitated this process by sending him to Thailand to immerse himself in the intricacies of the business. The strategic move was designed to cultivate Yashi’s confidence and expertise, encouraging him to take the reins when he felt ready. Yashi, driven by determination and a strong work ethic, embraced the opportunity wholeheartedly. His workaholic nature became evident as he dedicated himself to understanding the nuances of the company, setting the stage for his eventual leadership role in the family business.

Yashi's relentless work ethic, operating around the clock, took a toll on his health as he disregarded basic self-care. His indifference towards meals and well-being manifested in a spectrum of health issues, including anaemia, persistent diarrhea, continuous headaches, and occasional abnormal blood pressure. Astonishingly, Yashi seemed unfazed by these alarming symptoms, displaying a concerning neglect for his own health. It was during this period that I embarked on a journey to Thailand for my higher studies, driven not only by academic pursuits but also a passion for culinary arts. Fuelled by a love for cooking, I sought to immerse myself in the vibrant Thai culinary tradition while observing Yashi's health challenges with a growing sense of concern.

It was a delightful morning when Yashi, after a significant gap of years, arrived to pick me up at the airport. As I laid eyes on him, a wave of shock swept over me – he had become remarkably lean and thin. The transformation was so profound that I struggled to recognize the person I once knew. In that moment, a deep sense of concern and empathy enveloped me, realizing the toll his workaholic lifestyle had taken on him. Despite the surprise, I embraced him in a warm hug, unable to conceal my genuine sorrow for the visible impact on his well-being."

"I made it. Thanks for picking me up," I expressed as Yashi greeted me at the airport.

"Glad you are here. How was the trip?" Yashi inquired.

"Not bad, just a bit tiring. The flight was smooth though. Yashi, what happened to you? You became so lean," I questioned, noting the change in his appearance.

"It's because of the work, not a big deal. Ready to head home?" Yash asked, seemingly brushing off the concern.

“Absolutely, I’m a bit tired. Yashi, are you okay if I’m staying with you?” I inquired, aware of his preference for solitude.

“I don’t care because it’s you. I don’t like any others staying with me. I like to be alone,” Yash responded.

“Thank you, Yashi. Let me call my dad. Give me a sec,” I excused myself.

While calling my dad, Yashi listened to my conversation, wearing a smile.

“What is it? Why are you smiling?” I asked him.

“No, I was just going through the past. How is your dad, grandparents?” Yashi enquired.

“Yes, all are keeping well. Everyone asked to give their regards,” I shared.

“Okay,” he said, continuing the warm reunion between cousins who, despite no blood relation, shared a unique and cherished bond. As we headed home, the conversation flowed effortlessly, reigniting the familial connection that time and distance had momentarily dimmed.

"Upon reaching home, Yashi graciously toured me through all the rooms and assisted in placing my luggage in my designated space. Despite observing some signs of discomfort in his stomach, my jet lag-induced exhaustion took precedence, and I chose not to dwell on it.

Recognizing my need for rest, Yashi, ever considerate, took the initiative to order food for us to share. As we settled into the comforts of home, the subtle concerns about his well-being lingered, but for the moment, the focus was on recuperating from the journey and enjoying the warmth of familial surroundings.

By the time I woke up, Yashi was already gone, having headed to the office. Curious about our lunch plans, I called him to inquire.

"Don't wait for me, Sidhu. I can't make it," Yash responded, his voice carrying a hint of busyness.

Understanding his commitments, I acknowledged, "No worries, Yashi. Take your time at the office. We can catch up later."

"Thanks, Sidhu. I'll let you know when I'm free," Yash assured before ending the call. The understanding tone conveyed a mutual respect for each other's schedules, allowing flexibility in our plans.

As I finished my meal and began unpacking my belongings, the clock ticked to 9:30 PM, and Yash had yet to return home. Concerned, I decided to call him.

"Yes, Siddu, I'm on my way. I'm buying food. Do you want anything special?" Yash inquired, his voice filled with consideration.

"No, no, it's okay. Anything will do for me. Just come home safe," I reassured him.

"Yes, I will," he responded, and his words carried an emotional resonance that I could feel even through the phone. With a sense of relief and understanding, we concluded the conversation, anticipating Yash's safe return and the opportunity to share a meal together."

Yash's voice echoed through the house, calling out, 'Sidhu, where are you?' as he continued recording.

"Yes, coming," I swiftly replied, making my way to where he was."

CHAPTER IV

"Capturing Life's Symphony: A Story Unveiled"

On Day third of recording, Yash shared his voice, adding a beautiful touch to our project.

"Yashi, fancy checking out some markets or grocery spots tomorrow?" Sidharth asked.

"Sure thing, count me in," I replied.

"So when do your classes kick off?" I asked.

"Next week, starting the college grind," Sidhu answered.

"No worries, I'll show you around, the shops, and the shortcuts," I told him.

"Thanks a bunch, Yashi," Sidharth said appreciatively.

Grabbed some Pad Thai and Khao Pad for dinner...

"Seeing Sidhu enjoying the grub, I felt a wave of relief.

The next day, I took Sidhu to the nearby market where he got everything he needed. After loading up on essentials, we headed back home. On the way, I casually showed him my office, which conveniently happened to be close to our apartment. It's a small world around here.

After dropping Sidhu off, I made my way to the office. Meanwhile, Sidhu unpacked all the items he purchased and neatly arranged them in his own way. He must have realized that the kitchen is a territory I seldom venture into, except for the occasional coffee or drinks. It felt good to see him settling in comfortably.

He skilfully prepared our beloved Indian meal – rice with aromatic sambar and an array of flavourful curries. Sidhu, my thoughtful cousin, even took the effort to locate my office and surprised me by delivering a homemade lunch. The receptionist, recognizing him from our earlier introduction, warmly welcomed him into my workspace. Regrettably, I found myself in a sour mood that particular day."

"Yashi, this is your lunch for today," Sidhu shared with genuine enthusiasm.

"Take it back, Sidhu. I won't be in the office today during lunchtime," I responded with an unpleasant edge.

"Yashi, I understand you're incredibly busy, but I genuinely believe that enjoying a homemade lunch is essential. Can we find a way to make it work, even on your busiest days?" Sidharth spoke with a sincere concern.

"I simply don't have time for that! Why are you pushing this?" I asked, struggling to maintain my composure.

"I completely get it, and I don't want to add more stress. However, having a proper meal is crucial. Your well-being matters to me," Sidharth insisted, displaying genuine care.

"Can't you understand what I am saying?" I exclaimed, losing my patience. Inadvertently, my hand knocked the lunch box from Sidhu's grasp.

Sidharth was visibly disturbed by this unintentional act. Swiftly retrieving the dropped container, he uttered, "I'm sorry; I shouldn't have insisted or come."

Feeling remorseful for my behaviour, I found myself at a loss. As Sidharth was about to leave, I offered a sincere apology, "I'm sorry; I didn't mean it this way or to hurt you."

"It's okay. I understand," Sidhu said in a sad tone, attempting to put on a reassuring smile.

Feeling the weight of Sidhu's departure, my heart sank. Overwhelmed with regret, I acknowledged the gravity of my actions, whispering to myself, "No excuses, only apologies. I am truly sorry, Sidhu."

Drawing in a deep breath, I uttered, "I believe it's time to gracefully conclude for today. Our story, however, remains an ongoing masterpiece," concluding the recording with a reflective and poignant tone.

CHAPTER V

“Echoes of Empathy: A Tale of Friendship, Understanding, and Resilience”

On Day four, Sidharth’s voice enriched our story with simple yet beautiful nuances.

"Returning home after experiencing Yashi’s hurtful behaviour left me feeling emotionally shattered. Overwhelmed with distress, I found solace in tears, releasing the pent-up emotions like a vulnerable child. Coping with the unintentional pain was a challenging task, and in those moments, I deeply longed for the comforting presence of my dad, whose support I sorely missed.

While immersed in my upset feelings towards him, Yash reached out to me. Answering his call, I maintained silence as he called out, “Sidhu, Sidhu, are you listening?” Responding with a nonchalant “Hmmm,” I listened as he sincerely apologized for our earlier altercation.

Sensing his genuine regret, he proposed, “I know you’re mad at me. Shall we go for dinner, if you’re okay with it?”

Without hesitation, I agreed, saying, “Yes, I’ll go with you.” With that, our plans for dinner were settled.

Back home, if Yash was visiting with his parents for vacations, it was almost a certainty that he would find himself grounded for trivial reasons. Despite this, I remained a supportive presence in his life. One incident vividly etched in my memory reflects his rebellion over a lunch that didn’t suit his taste.

Unwilling to conform, Yash faced the consequence of his actions as his mom, disapproving of his behaviour, grounded him. He was escorted to a room and left in solitude, the door firmly locked as a stern reminder of the repercussions of his choices.

In those moments, I stood by him, understanding that everyone has their quirks and preferences.

Positioned near the window, I sat beneath it, offering solace to Yash during his time of grounding. My heart went out to him, and a persistent sense of sympathy lingered within me. Frequently, I found myself questioning my own father about the strictness Yash endured from his parents, puzzled by their lack of understanding.

Grateful for my dad's unwavering support and kindness, I often thanked him for being the antithesis of Yash's parents. My dad, a superlative figure, evoked deep love and admiration within me, contrasting starkly with the challenging dynamics Yash faced in his own family.

Despite Yash's anguished shouts commanding me to leave, I remained steadfast by his side. Seated beside him, I attempted to comfort him by singing soothing songs. In a small gesture to lift his spirits, I drew a Spider-Man illustration and passed it through the window. However, he reacted with frustration, tearing the drawing into pieces and unleashing another outburst of anger in my direction.

Witnessing this emotional turmoil, my dad intervened, approaching the window to address Yash directly. With a gentle yet firm tone, he implored, "Yashi, you know that I love you just like I love Sidhu. Please, stop shouting at him."

Yash, his heart heavy with sorrow, met my father's gaze, tears streaming down his face. In response to my dad's plea, he reluctantly retreated to his bed, enveloped in his own emotional struggle.

My dad persisted in his attempt to bridge the emotional gap between Yash and me. “Yashi, he’s just a kid. Despite his own sadness, he’s here to support you. Why can’t you accept it? He’s offering you his shoulders for you to lean on, to find relaxation and calmness. Can’t you understand, Yashi?”

Yash, grappling with his emotions, approached the window, holding my dad’s hand as tears rolled down his face. “Uncle, I’m not in the mood. Please understand,” he pleaded. The poignant scene unfolded, a painful moment for both my dad and me, as we witnessed the struggle of emotions between a young friend in need and the challenges of understanding and accepting that support.

“You can always lean on either of our shoulders whenever you’re sad or mad at anything. Stop crying for now,” my dad reassured Yash.

“Why are my parents so strict, Uncle? I’m totally fed up with them,” Yash expressed, his heartbroken tone revealing the weight of his frustration.

“Relax, my child. Everything is going to be alright. I promise,” my dad comforted him.

Gradually, Yash settled down, taking a seat beneath the window, next to me. Engaging in a meaningful conversation, we discussed various topics, sharing laughter and finding happiness in the process. Meanwhile, my dad bought Yash’s favourite meals, creating a comforting atmosphere that helped uplift our spirits, bringing a sense of joy to the day.

Understanding Yash’s nature, I recognized that it wasn’t his fault; rather, the challenging circumstances around him shaped his demeanour. Despite the complexities, I never harboured anger toward him.

Confident that he would eventually find solace and settle with me, I embraced patience and understanding. This unwavering belief in our friendship brought me a sense of happiness, knowing that I was there for him in times of need."

As the recording came to a halt, a contemplative sentiment lingered. Reflecting on the shared experiences and the hope for a future video, I acknowledged the bond we had and the anticipation for the day we could capture our moments in a visual dialogue. The promise of a future video call added a layer of anticipation, marking the end of the conversation for today.

CHAPTER VI

"Unexpected Gestures: Nourishing the Heart and Soul"

Yash's voiceover on Day five. painted simplicity with a brush of beauty, creating an enchanting audio masterpiece.

During our dinner outing, I harboured a desire to ask Sindhu to continue bringing me lunch every day, but fear held me back. The apprehension lingered, casting a shadow over the entire evening, making it feel like a day fraught with doom.

The following morning, Sidhu mentioned a nearby gym and expressed his intention to check it out.

"Yashi, I need workouts. I'm planning to visit the nearby gym and see the schedule," Sidharth said.

"Okay," I replied, a tinge of sadness creeping into my mind, wondering why he didn't inquire if I was interested. After a moment's reflection, I realized it might be related to the lunch box incident, perhaps an intentional avoidance to sidestep any awkwardness.

I got ready, and by the time I was set, Sidhu had prepared breakfast. It wasn't a regular occurrence for me, but when he takes charge of the kitchen, I find it impossible to resist. His culinary creations are nothing short of exceptional, with flavours that are undeniably mouth-watering. I have developed a genuine love for his cooking, each dish a testament to his skill and the undeniable pleasure that comes from savouring his delicious meals.

We shared a delightful breakfast together.

"Yashi, how's the breakfast? Do you like it?" Sidharth inquired with a warm smile.

"Yes, it's absolutely delicious. Having you here adds an extra touch to the flavours," I replied appreciatively.

Sidharth graced me with a delightful smile, and as he nodded, a gentle "hmmm..." escaped his lips, adding a touch of serene beauty to the moment.

" Are you busy today?" Sidharth asked, his tone genuine.

"Yes, quite occupied. Any particular reason you're asking?" I inquired curiously.

"No reason, just checking," Sidhu replied casually.

Despite the unspoken desire to bring up the topic of lunch, a lingering apprehension held me back, leaving the words unsaid in the air between us.

Surprisingly, during my office routine, the receptionist called out, "Sir, your cousin left a lunchbox for you," adding an unexpected and delightful twist to the day.

"What?" I asked, astonishment colouring my voice. My happiness soared.

"Ask him to wait; I am coming," I eagerly requested.

"I'm sorry, Sir. He already left," the receptionist regretfully replied.

"He left? Okay then, thank you," I disconnected, a tinge of sadness settling in. I immediately called Sidharth.

"Hello," Sidhu answered.

"Why did you leave like that?" I inquired, genuinely puzzled.

"I wanted to avoid hurting myself again, that's all," Sidharth explained.

"I promised I wouldn't repeat it. Why this?" I asked, a hint of sadness in my tone.

"Yashi, please don't take it to heart. I won't stop caring, even if you get angry. But remember, I have feelings too.

I just don't want to impose on you," Sidharth replied with sincerity.

"Okay, I understand," I said, disconnecting with a heavy heart. Later, I messaged him, "The food was delicious. Loved it."

He responded with a smiling emoji and said, "Thank you, happy that you enjoyed it." I sent a heart emoji, and he replied with a smiley.

"Sidhu, I never expected you'd prepare lunch for me again. I'm so happy. Thank you once again," I expressed my gratitude.

Sidharth responded with a heart emoji and messaged" you are always special for me". I chuckled and replied with a smiley.

Overwhelmed, I silently expressed in my mind, "I've never felt cared for like this before. Thank you, Sidhu."

As the day's recording drew to a close, I concluded with a profound sense of newfound joy and deep appreciation for the unexpected gestures of kindness that had illuminated my day.

Sidhu's thoughtful act had not only filled my stomach but also touched my heart, leaving an enduring warmth that transcended the simple exchange of a lunchbox. Grateful for the connection and the genuine care extended my way, I savoured the moment, reflecting on how small gestures can have a profound impact on our emotional well-being.

CHAPTER VII

“In the Wake of Wellness”

Day six of recording embraced Yash’s voice, filling the studio with a beautiful simplicity that resonated effortlessly.

"The next day, a loud bang echoed through my door, rousing me from my sleep. With a yawn, I opened the door to find Sidhu standing there.

“What is it, Sidhu?” I asked in my still sleepy state.

“Come on, get ready in 10 minutes. We are going to the gym,” Sidhu replied.

“What? Why me? I’m not interested; I want to sleep a little longer,” I protested.

“Come on, Yashi, you’ve got to give the gym a shot with me. It’s high time we kick laziness to the curb,” Sidharth urged.

“I’m really not into the whole gym thing,” I insisted.

“Look, I get it. But imagine the gains we’ll make together, the energy boost, and the overall sense of accomplishment. You won’t regret it,” Sidharth insisted.

“I just don’t think it’s my thing,” I reiterated.

“Alright, how about this – we’ll start with a light workout, take it slow. It’s not about becoming a fitness fanatic overnight. We’ll make it as easy as possible for you,” Sidhu suggested.

“I still don’t know,” I hesitated.

“Listen, I need your support on this, and I promise you won’t be alone in this journey. We’ll be gym buddies, cheering each other on. Plus, think of the positive impact on our health,” Sidhu persisted.

"I don't want to feel forced into it," I replied.

"Fair enough. But just imagine how proud we'll be of ourselves after a few sessions. I'm not taking no for an answer – let's do this together," Sidhu encouraged.

"Alright, alright... fine... I'll give it a try. Wait for me... are you happy?" I agreed with hesitation as I had no other choice.

"That's the spirit! You won't regret it, and soon you'll thank me for pushing you. We're going to crush it at the gym!" Sidhu exclaimed with infectious enthusiasm.

I smiled while closing the door and thanked him in my mind for considering me.

In a matter of minutes, we ventured off to the gym, and the experience of working out was surprisingly enjoyable, especially alongside someone as cherished as Sidhu.

On our way back, curiosity got the better of me, and I questioned Sidhu, "Why did you insist on dragging me to the gym?"

"Oh, that... I just don't want to see you unwell in your prime, you workaholic," Sidhu expressed sincerely. "I genuinely mean it, Yashi. I want you to be healthy, at least for me."

His words struck a chord, and I gazed at him emotionally, inquiring, "Why do you care about me this much? My parents never did this, if my memory serves me right."

"And you've got the answer right there. From now on, you have me. Whatever it is, you can rely on me," Sidhu assured with a warm smile.

Tears welled up in my eyes as I went through a wave of emotions. Sidhu playfully teased me, calling me "crying Yashi."

“Yashi, our dinner is ready. Come, let’s have it together,” came Sidhu’s message.

“Yes, coming,” I replied, and as I wrap up my recording, I couldn’t help but feel grateful for the unexpected bond that had blossomed."

CHAPTER VIII

"Silent Resonance: Nurturing Bonds and Breaking Habits"

On the seventh day of recording, Sidharth's voice flowed gracefully, infusing the studio with a simple and beautiful cadence.

"Yashi was visibly emotional after our gym session. It's clear he needed the workout. I've decided to join him on this journey to help him break free from the grip of neglecting his health.

His workaholic tendencies worry me, and I want him to prioritize his well-being. If I'm not there to encourage him, I fear he'll revert to his old habits.

The gym sessions aren't just about physical fitness; they're my attempt to alleviate his persistent headaches. It's been a week since I arrived, and I've noticed his struggle. I've been messaging his head every night, but in my absence, he resorts to painkillers.

I'm determined to bring about positive change. Why am I doing this? Honestly, I don't have a straightforward answer. There's just something about Yashi that draws me in more than anyone else in the world," Sidharth shared, a smile playing on his lips as he reflected on his thoughts.

"Sidhu," Yashi knocked at the door.

"Yes, Yashi, come in," I welcomed him.

"What were you recording?" Yashi inquired.

"It's just my thoughts. Do you want to hear?" I asked.

"Of course, yes. I'd love to," Yashi replied.

"Promise me not to ask any questions," I insisted.

"Yes, I promise," Yashi assured.

I played the recording for him, and he eagerly listened, smiling. Observing the way he absorbed my words brought me joy.

After the recording, we exchanged smiles. Yashi gently kissed my forehead and embraced me tightly. Our mutual understanding of emotions eliminated the need for many words.

In that moment, silence spoke volumes, and we basked in the beauty of our connection.

CHAPTER IX

"Harmonies of Joy: A Melodic Journey of Friendship and Passion"

In the recording studio on Day eight, Sidharth's voice painted a beautiful melody with a simple yet profound touch.

"I couldn't help but notice Yash's violin sitting idle. I wanted to reignite his passion for it and share the joy of music in my upcoming recording."

I found myself pondering ways to reignite Yash's passion for the violin. Struggling for ideas, I decided to give a simple yet special approach, a try.

I prepared some dishes for him and eagerly waited. Upon his arrival, he caught me playing with his cherished violin, a possession he rarely allows others to touch. However, I seemed to be an exception.

Though he didn't utter a word, a smile spoke volumes as he headed to freshen up. Meanwhile, I continued experimenting with dissonant notes on the violin.

When Yash returned, he gently held my hands, and together we created a harmonious melody. It was an unforgettable moment," Sidharth reminisced with a smile.

Spotting Yashi next to me during the recording, I exclaimed in surprise, "Yashi, I didn't know you were here."

"Hmm," Yashi responded, "I noticed. You forgot to close the door."

I giggled, "Is that so?"

Yashi, with a smile, asked, "Shall I continue with what you were recommending?"

"So you heard," I inquired.

"Hmm," he nodded affirmatively. I handed over the microphone to Yashi and sat beside him, savouring the beauty of his words.

"Sidhu appreciated me, acknowledging that I hadn't forgotten it yet, and the experience was amazing. As we played together, I could see the joy in Sidhu's eyes, his spirit illuminated.

Curious, Sidharth asked, 'Why don't you play while I sing?' Intrigued by the idea, I agreed. Sidharth began singing "Nagumo Omu Ganaleni," and I started playing the violin. The music flowed effortlessly between us, blending into a marvelous fusion. In that moment, we both lost ourselves in the magic of music, our souls intertwined with the melody. It was a moment of pure joy and harmony, a testament to the beauty of shared passions.

I have a video clip of that enchanting performance on my phone, and I'll be adding it to this video soon."

"What do you think, Sidhu?" I inquired.

Sidharth replied, "Yes, that will be wonderful."

From that day onwards, whenever we found ourselves with free time, we indulged in creating musical fusions like the one that brought us joy initially. The experience was immensely enjoyable, becoming a cherished routine for us. We decided to continue this harmonious tradition, weaving melodies together whenever the opportunity presented itself.

Concluding the recording session for today, I paused and gracefully stopped the recording. The stories shared, the music created, and the memories woven together formed a beautiful narrative. With a sense of contentment, I looked forward to revisiting these moments and crafting more tales in the future.

CHAPTER X

"Bridges Beyond Borders: Navigating College Life in Bangkok Through Friendship and Flavourful Encounters"

On the ninth day of recording, the studio resonated with beauty as Sidharth's voice set the stage, harmonizing seamlessly with Yash, creating a melodic duet that enchanted the senses.

"My college journey began with a mix of excitement and nerves. The campus buzzed with an invigorating atmosphere, filled with the tempting aroma of street food. Thailand's lively spirit embraced me, setting the stage for adventures in this new chapter. Alongside my business management studies, exploring Thai cuisine adds a flavourful twist to my college life.

In the busy surroundings, I navigated unfamiliar terrain. Napat, a friendly Thai student, offered a hand for the campus tour with a beaming smile. Despite his great English, cultural differences led to laughter as we tried to understand Thai customs.

Exploring Thailand's food scene was a fun challenge. Mixing up spicy and sweet, and my clumsy chopstick attempts kept my new friends entertained.

Learning Thai street food with classmates strengthened our friendship. Laughter filled the air at aromatic stalls, turning markets into classrooms. These culinary adventures enriched my palate and created lasting connections.

Those days of joy and simplicity are dearly missed, and looking back brings a wave of nostalgic memories.

Our home was always buzzing with friends, gathering nearly every weekend for catch-ups. They loved the food I cooked, and we shared moments of joy with small refreshments. Initially, Yashi found it a bit annoying, but over time, he became an integral part of our group. Together, we embraced the fun and enjoyment that radiated from our shared experiences."

Sidharth, with a camera in hand, poised to capture the essence of that day forever. Every frame telling a story, freezing time in a perfect blend of memories. “Those were the days, and oh, how I long to relive them.”

A gentle smile adorned Sidharth’s face as he took a slow, contemplative breath, inhaling the fleeting beauty of the moment with a serene exhale.

CHAPTER XI

"Echoes of Connection: Melodies, Moments, and Deepening Bonds"

As Day ten unfolded in the recording studio, Sidharth's voice filled the space, creating a simple and beautiful composition that lingered in the echoes.

"Being a part of the cultural fest in college was an incredible experience. Ankitha, Yash, and I decided to do a special performance together, and we chose the song "Endoru mahanu bhavulu" The collaboration turned out to be a huge success, and the energy from the audience was electrifying.

Shortly before the fest, Ankitha visited with her Singaporean boyfriend, adding an extra layer of excitement. To accommodate her stay, she ended up at our apartment, where Yash and I welcomed her. It was great having her around, and to make her stay comfortable, I decided to give up my room temporarily, moving into Yash's room.

It's these unexpected moments that make college life unforgettable, and the bond we shared during the cultural fest created memories that will last a lifetime.

Sharing a room with Yashi brought us closer in ways I hadn't expected. One evening, he opened up and shared some deeply personal and sad moments from his life, making himself vulnerable. As he poured out his emotions, I instinctively held him tightly, offering comfort as he cried.

Witnessing Yashi's pain made me feel a profound sadness for him, realizing he had been carrying this burden alone until that day. This newfound vulnerability deepened my feelings for him, and I began to care for him even more. Our bond strengthened as he trusted me with his emotions, and from that day forward, he felt comfortable sharing everything with me.

Building such a strong connection with Yashi was a meaningful experience. The more he opened up, the more I felt the need to be there for him. This shared vulnerability allowed me to understand him better, fostering a friendship built on trust, support, and genuine care.

Alright then, wrapping up for today. It's been a journey sharing stories and memories. If you ever want to dive back into these conversations or explore something new, I'll be right here. Until next time, take care and see you around."

CHAPTER XII

"Whispers of Strength: A Tapestry of Challenges, Unbreakable Bonds, and Shared Triumphs"

On the eleventh day of recording, Yash's weary voice narrated a challenging chapter in his life.

"Burdened by a demanding work project and the added pressure from my dad, I found myself at the intersection of exhaustion and overwhelming stress. Yearning for a moment of respite,I expressed a deep desire to be invisible, to escape the relentless challenges I faced. In the midst of this struggle, my fatigue and emotional strain were palpable, underscoring the gravity of the situation I found myself in.

During that crucial moment, Sidhu answered a call from my dad, unaware that it wasn't me on the line, leading to an unconditional scolding. "Uncle, this is Sidharth. I'll have him call you back; he's in the shower," Sidharth calmly responded.

"Ah, Sidharth, how are you, son?" my dad inquired. "I'm good, hope you are too. Regards to Aunt and Ankitha," Sudhu conveyed.

"Yes, just ask him to call me back," my dad instructed before the call disconnected. As Sidhu turned back, I emerged from the bathroom, the unexpected twist in the conversation adding a touch of irony to the challenging day.

"Why is your face so pale? Who were you talking to?" I anxiously inquired.

"Yashi, I've always been here. Why face the pressure and your dad's scolding alone at twenty-seven? You have my shoulders. Did I vanish or something? Why doesn't your dad trust you?" Sidhu questioned with a simple beauty, approaching gently, a genuine friend in every word.

"Sidhu," I softly called him, overwhelmed. I embraced him tightly, unable to contain my emotions.

"I hate your dad," Sidhu confessed while hugging me, and I couldn't help but chuckled.

"I'm sorry, I didn't share because I didn't want to burden you. I'm sorry I kept it from you," I apologized.

"Yashi, do you trust me?" Sidhu asked, and I replied, "Yes, a hundred percent."

"Assign me some work; we'll do it together. I know what you're going to say. Please don't say a thing. We'll finish it together. Do you agree?" Sidhu proposed.

"Hmm... yes, we can do it together," I agreed, finding solace in the shared commitment to face the challenges ahead.

Amidst the relentless pressure, our collaboration became a seamless dance of support, each of us aiding the other in overcoming obstacles, leading to shared success.

In the aftermath of that challenging day, a resolute determination settled within me like a quiet vow. Come what may, I pledged to hold his hand tightly, an unwavering grip that would defy any attempt to take him away from me.

He, who consistently stood by my side as a steadfast pillar of support, always equipped with a compassionate ear and genuine empathy, had become my silver lining. In the tempest of life's storms, he remained a constant source of strength, an anchor grounding me through every trial and tribulation.

As we relaxed at the apex of our apartment, I gazed at Sidhu, a beer can in my hand, reflecting on this newfound understanding. Lost in my thoughts, I looked up to find him smiling, his eyes filled with warmth, mirroring the peaceful contentment that settled between us. An evening adorned with shared smiles, overlooking the traffic below, became a testament to the beauty that blossomed from our unwavering connection."

As the day drew to a close, The microphone silenced, marking the end of today's chapter, encapsulating a narrative rich with emotional highs and lows, leaving behind a recorded testament to the journey navigated, with its twists, turns, and the unwavering support of those who played pivotal roles in the narrative of my life.

CHAPTER XIII

"Celebrating Bonds: Echoes of Success in the Journey Together"

On Recording Day twelve, amidst the hustle and bustle of our professional and academic pursuits, Sidharth and I unearthed a profound strength in reveling in each other's triumphs.

"Allow me to guide you through a recent chapter in our story—a narrative that echoes with success and camaraderie. [Yash 's voice over.]

It all commenced with a triumphant moment at the office, a project that demanded dedication and innovation. Navigating the intricacies of professional challenges, Sidharth's genuine joy not only amplified the victory but added a layer of shared accomplishment to our tale.

In the glow of my professional achievement, enhanced by Sidharth's invaluable support, the narrative seamlessly transitions to the academic realm. Sidharth's successful completion of two challenging semesters, Becomes a poignant story of perseverance and unwavering commitment. As I recount these shared victories, I can't help but emphasize the resonance of our celebrations—echoing beyond the confines of workspaces and classrooms, reinforcing the profound depth of our bond.

Our journey unfolds, underscoring the significance of mutual joy and support. It's not merely about hitting milestones; it's about those shared moments of triumph that sculpt our unique camaraderie. Whether in the office or academia, each success intricately weaves into the narrative of our bond. In the tapestry of our friendship, shared celebrations stand out as pivotal moments, fortifying the bonds between Sidharth and me.

As I narrate, you'll hear the echoes of a relationship that goes beyond the surface—nurtured by the genuine happiness found in each other's accomplishments.

Reflecting on our joint journey, the story delves into the intricacies of a friendship that has weathered professional storms and academic challenges. Shared victories become markers of growth, reinforcing the foundations of our connection—a story of resilience and understanding, where success intertwines our lives.

Looking ahead, the story anticipates more chapters of shared victories, endurance and celebrations. My voice resonates with optimism, knowing that the strengthened bond between us will continue to be a guiding force. In this tale of companionship, each success becomes a beautiful stepping stone, propelling Sidharth and me forward with the assurance that we have a companion to celebrate and support at every turn."

CHAPTER XIV

" Mirthful Mall Moments and Serendipitous Encounters"

On Day thirteen of recording, Sidharth's voice graced the studio with an effortless charm, creating a melody that felt like a soothing breeze on a serene day.

"Yash and I decided to hit the mall for some casual shopping. As we strolled through the aisles, Yash picked up a neon-coloured shirt, and I couldn't help but tease him, saying, "Yashi, you trying to blind people with that choice?"

Yash shot back, "At least I won't get lost in a crowd!"

We both burst into laughter, drawing some curious glances from other shoppers. Undeterred, Yash grabbed a pair of funky sunglasses, exclaiming, "These will match the shirt perfectly!"

I chimed in, "Are you auditioning for a role in a Bollywood sci-fi movie?"

Yash responded with an exaggerated Bollywood pose, and we couldn't stop laughing. Suddenly, a salesperson approached us, trying to promote the latest fragrance.

Sidharth, in his deep voice, deadpanned, "Do you have a scent that makes bad jokes smell better?"

The salesperson chuckled nervously, realizing they had stumbled upon a pair of mischief-makers. Yash and I left the store, still laughing about our unexpected comedy show

.

From there, we headed to purchase a new microphone for recording. As we were about to complete the transaction at the counter, my dad's call interrupted the moment. Without hesitation, I excused myself from Yash and stepped out of the shop to take the call. However, in the midst of this, an unforeseen twist occurred as I inadvertently collided with a group of girls passing by.

The sudden Impact caused my phone to slip from my grasp, landing on the floor. In those brief moments of surprise and fluster, I swiftly recovered my phone.

" I'm so sorry," I offered my apologies to the girls.

"Are you Sidharth?" inquired one of the girls.

"Indeed, that's me. How do you know?" I responded.

"I'm from the same college, a literature student. I noticed you during a special performance on Arts Day. It was truly fantastic. We thoroughly enjoyed it," she shared.

"Thank you. Could I know your name?" I asked politely.

"I'm Riya. I'm also from India," she replied with a warm smile.

"Oh, I see." While our conversation continued, Yash emerged from the shop. I introduced Riya to him, and vice versa.

"We're just about to grab lunch. Would you like to join us?" Yash invited.

"Thanks, but not this time. We have other plans," Riya gracefully declined, and we bid each other farewell.

I quickly called my dad, explaining the unexpected situation. We engaged in a heartfelt conversation, both of us sharing the day's events and catching up on each other's lives. With a sense of reassurance, we concluded the call and continued our respective journeys within the bustling surroundings.

It was downright comical how these girls seemed genuinely stunned by our supposedly handsome looks. Yash and I couldn't help but burst into laughter, finding their reaction more amusing than flattering. The whole day turned out to be just awesome – a perfect moment filled with laughter and unexpected fun."

CHAPTER XV

"Silent Vow: The Unspoken Symphony of Love"

On the fourteenth day of recording, Sidharth's voice flowed through the studio, weaving a beautiful narrative that intertwined with the melodies, leaving an enchanting echo in its wake.

"That evening, as I busied myself with dinner preparations, Yashi arrived with a small box.

"What's inside?" I inquired, curiosity tingling in my voice.

"Open it and see for yourself," Yashi responded with a hint of excitement.

I opened the box, revealing a couple's chain, one with an "S" locket and the other with a "Y" locket.

"Wow, it's beautiful," I exclaimed, reaching for it. But before I could, he closed the box and asked, "Do you like it?"

"Of course, I do," I replied, anticipation building.

"Sidhu," he called me with affection, prompting my full attention.

"Hmmm," I responded, my heart racing.

Yashi's gaze met mine, and in that silent exchange, I felt a question linger between us, unspoken yet palpable. The air around us seemed to hold its breath, waiting for the moment to unfold. It was as if his eyes were asking for something more, something deeper than words could convey.

"Amidst the quiet whispers of the evening breeze and the gentle caress of moonlight, I find myself drawn to you, captivated by the warmth of your presence. In this moment, as our souls intertwine in the dance of fate, I am compelled to ask: would you grace me with the privilege of being not just a companion, but a keeper of your heart? Will you allow me to journey with you through life's joys and sorrows, hand in hand, as we paint the canvas of our shared dreams with the vibrant hues of our love?"

Yashi whispered, his words imbued with tender affection, lingering in the air, inviting a moment of heartfelt connection.

The weight of the moment lingered, filling the room with anticipation. As the revelation unfolded, leaving me momentarily astonished, I felt the weight of the profound question hanging in the air. Regaining consciousness, I bridged the emotional chasm between us, sealing our unspoken bond with a tender kiss.

In the exquisite intimacy of our lip lock, words became obsolete, replaced by the raw authenticity of our shared emotions. That kiss served as the eloquent proclamation of my answer, a silent vow that transcended spoken language—a testament to the profound connection forged in that sacred moment.

Yashi delicately placed the Chain on my neck, and an overwhelming sense of joy enveloped me. In the midst of this bliss, we shared a tender lip lock, the intensity of our connection growing. The burner was extinguished, and with a subtle touch, Yash led me to his bed, setting the stage for an unforgettable journey.

In the intimate confines of his bedroom, a series of passionate lip locks unfolded. The gradual removal of our clothes mirrored the deepening connection between us.

With each intimate kiss, Yash explored every inch of my being, leaving no space untouched. The air was charged with anticipation as we embarked on a journey, sharing the intimacy of our bodies for the first time.

As the night unfolded, we found ourselves in the embrace of a shared shower, a cascade of water enhancing the sensuality of the moment. The shower became a canvas for more lip locks and deep kisses, the water droplets echoing the rhythm of our shared desire. Each moment was savoured, and the bond between us deepened with every touch, creating memories that lingered in the air.

In the quiet aftermath, a profound sense of satisfaction lingered. We had enjoyed each moment, weaving a tapestry of shared experiences that transcended the physical. The echoes of our passion resonated, leaving us with a memory of a night where joy, connection, and intimacy converged in perfect harmony, destined to be imprinted in the deepest recesses of our hearts, a thrilling emotional crescendo that would resonate through time."

As the fourteenth day of recording came to a close, Sidharth wrapped up with a smile, leaving behind a studio filled with the echoes of a perfect day captured in his voice.

CHAPTER XVI

"Fractured Moments, Enduring Love: A Chronicle of Challenges and Devotion"

On the fifteenth day of recording, Yashi and Sidharth joined the session. The narrative begins with Sidharth's voice taking the lead.

"On the following day, Yashi wasn't feeling well, his stomach upset from the previous day's food and had a slight fever.

"Yashi, please take a day off and rest at home. I'll whip up some soothing porridge for you, and there's ORS next to the flask. Make sure to stay hydrated," I urged.

"Yes," Yashi agreed.

"I'll swing by the pharmacy for some meds before heading to college," I assured.

"Hmmm," Yashi softly replied.

After obtaining the medication, I handed it to him, ensuring he was cared for, before making my way back to college.

During my break, I received a message from Yashi, "Sidhu, got a call from the office, had to rush. Don't worry, I'm much better. I promise I'll be back soon. I'm sorry, Sidhu."

Concerned, I called Yashi, but he was unreachable. I promptly messaged him, expressing my intent to come to his location.

Taking swift action, I called for a taxi and headed towards Yashi's place, determined to check on him in person.

Approaching Yashi's workplace, the familiar bustle of the city faded into the background as a truck came hurtling into view, its massive frame careening out of control. My heart leaped into my throat as I realized the imminent danger. With a surge of urgency, I shouted at the driver to halt our vehicle, but it was too late.

The truck's monstrous form collided with three cars, including the one I was traveling in. The impact was shattering, metal screeching against metal, glass shattering like fragile dreams. The world spun in a sickening whirlwind of chaos and destruction.

When the dust settled, the scene before me was a nightmare incarnate. The once peaceful street was now a tableau of tragedy, twisted metal and broken glass scattered like morbid confetti.

Five lives were lost in that heart-wrenching moment, their stories abruptly ended, leaving behind a void that could never be filled. And I, too, lay amidst the wreckage, unconscious, my own fate hanging in the balance.

Observing the difficulty in Yashi's expression, I sensed he found it challenging to discuss the events of that day. Leaning towards him, I tightly held his hand for support.

"Yashi, I'm right here beside you. Take your time and share what you want to say," I reassured him, sealing the sentiment with a gentle kiss on his cheek."

CHAPTER XVII

"Resilience Rewritten: A Journey Through Adversity and the Power of Love"

In his voiceover, Yash recounted the traumatic incident that deeply affected him on the same day.

"After completing my work, I glanced at my phone, discovering missed calls and a message from Sidhu. Upon returning the call, a police inspector answered, revealing the unsettling news and disclosing the hospital details.

A moment of breathlessness enveloped me, rendering me numb. Somehow, I regained composure, tears streaming down my face. Urgently, I contacted my assistant, imploring him to drive me to the hospital, as the gravity of the news left me too shattered to navigate the journey alone.

Sidhu suffered a traumatic head injury, necessitating immediate attention upon our arrival at the hospital. Rushed into surgery due to swelling and bleeding, the procedure loomed as a major undertaking. In the midst of uncertainty, I found myself grappling with the ordeal, uncertain of how I would endure. A wave of relief washed over me only when the doctor confirmed the success of the surgery, finally allowing my breath to return to a normal rhythm.

He remained unconscious, confined to the ICU. Gazing at him through the glass, I grappled with the uncertainty of when he would regain consciousness. Once settled, I mustered the strength to call his father, narrating the harrowing events. The next day, his father arrived at the hospital, witnessing Sidharth's condition. For the ensuing two days, he stood by my side, providing support and comfort. Eventually, he left, entrusting Sidharth to my care, withholding the distressing news from our grandparents.

"He spent three agonizing months in the hospital. It was only after this long, arduous wait that they finally allowed me a brief entry into the ICU. Every day, as I stood by his side, I would tell him, '"Sidhu, even in your sleep, you're my anchor. You mean everything to me, and I can't fathom a life without you by my side. Wake up soon, for you are my silver lining in every moment.'"

[These words, captured in the midst of a recording, brought a halt to Yash's voice, his emotions evident in the trembling tone. As Sidharth wiped away tears from his cheeks, the weight of those sentiments hung in the air.]

"Sidhu," I called out as he opened his eyes after three agonizing months of surgery. Overwhelmed with emotion, I burst into tears.

With a soft touch of my lips on his cheek, I whispered, my voice quivering with emotion, "Thank you for being my miracle. I cherish you more than words can convey, and I love you with every beat of my heart." In response, he mustered a tired smile, conveying a depth of emotion beyond words.

Eager to share the joy, I rushed to the nurse to spread the news. Doctors and nurses quickly gathered, examining him with a mix of relief and congratulations. The doctors commended his bravery, acknowledging the significance of him regaining consciousness. The room was filled with emotions, gratitude, and a shared sense of triumph over adversity.

I called Sidharth's dad to convey the wonderful news that his son had regained consciousness. Overjoyed, he expressed his gratitude and relief, his voice filled with emotion. Without wasting a moment, he promised to rush to the hospital first thing in the morning to see Sidharth. The love and concern in his words were palpable, a testament to the deep bond between father and son. It was a moment of pure joy and hope, a testament to the resilience of the human spirit."

CHAPTER XVIII

(2)"Resilience Rewritten: A Journey Through Adversity and the Power of Love"

Yash's recording unfolded, delving deeper into the harrowing details of the dreadful event that had left an enduring impact on him.

"We were both incredibly fortunate that Sidharth received the right treatment at the right time," Yash expressed with deep gratitude. "Thank you, Sidharth, for fighting so hard to return to a normal life. Thank you for being alive. Thank you for living alongside me." Yash sealed his sentiments with a tender kiss on Sidharth's forehead.

"After three months in hospital, Sidharth entered rehab for a month, ultimately emerging into a semblance of normalcy. Yash expressed gratitude to the heavens for this outcome.

During our coffee moment at the hospital cafeteria, Uncle Rohit's tearful eyes reflected the pain etched in his heart. "Twice my world shattered—first, when his parents perished in that car crash, and now, with this accident," he shared, his voice trembling with an emotional undercurrent.

As we delved into Sidharth's past, Uncle Rohit painted a canvas of beautiful memories from Sidhu's youth. We both cherished those moments, sharing smiles amid the heaviness of the situation.

Uncle Rohit's voice trembled with emotion as he recounted the heartfelt conversation with Sidharth. "When

Sidharth was young, the only time I was left speechless was when he asked about his mother. One day, he confronted me, accusing me of always finding excuses to avoid his questions about her. I didn't have the courage to tell him the truth, that I'm not his biological dad. As the years passed, he stopped asking, and I thought it was for the best. But one day, as he lay on my lap, he opened up and said, 'Dad, do you know why I stopped asking about my mom?' 'No,' I replied. 'Do you remember the day you asked me to take a document from your locker and give it to Mr. Samuel?' Sidharth said. 'That day, I not only saw the document you mentioned but also the confidential documents about my whereabouts."

I was momentarily stunned when I heard this. Sidharth continued, "Dad, thank you for not telling me what happened. Thank you for raising me as your own son and giving me all the privileges. I only want to live as your son." Overwhelmed with emotion, tears streamed down my face, but Sidharth remained strong. He comforted me, saying, 'You are the best dad I ever got. I'm so proud that I'm your son.'

In that tender moment, Sidharth's words resonated with a profound maturity, a depth of understanding that touched my heart. As he refused the picture of his parents, his words echoed with a poignant simplicity, "Dad, you are my everything. I only want you. Please allow me to be your son forever. I love you, Dad."

His sentiment struck me deeply, revealing the unwavering strength of our bond. With tears in my eyes, I embraced him tightly, whispering my consent. In that exchange, I realized the depth of his love and the unbreakable connection between us.

"Sidhu," I said, moved by his words, "you should keep this photo. It's a reminder of your parents' love and sacrifice, even in the toughest of times. I will always be your dad, and you will always be my son. Nothing in this world can change that."

With a gentle touch, I handed him the photo, knowing that it would serve as a symbol of his past, a beacon guiding him towards a future filled with love and resilience.

"I wish I could stand by him now, but circumstances..." Uncle Rohit's voice trailed off, and I reached out, whispering, "Uncle, don't bear this burden alone. I'll do everything in my power for him. The weight of regret from the accident rests heavily on my heart."

With a comforting touch, Uncle Rohit said, "It's his fate, and let's be grateful he's okay." Emotions welled up, and I confessed , "He's the anchor of my joy. In his presence, I've found transformation—a warmth, a positive light that defines my existence."

Uncle Rohit nodded, understanding the depth of our connection. "He cared for you, loved you deeply. His empathy came from witnessing your hardships. Because of him, you receive our monthly calls."

As I braced myself to admit I couldn't fathom life without him, Uncle Rohit's phone rang, interrupting the moment. We returned to the room, missing the chance, but the lingering emotional bond held us together in our shared concern and love for Sidhu."

As Sidhu's dad shared the details, Sidharth expressed, "I'm sorry for causing you and Yashi worry." His dad, with genuine warmth, reassured him, "Sidhu, it wasn't your fault. I'm grateful you're alive for both me and Yashi."

Sidharth mustered up his courage and decided to reveal his relationship with Yash to his dad, seeking acceptance.

With a deep breath, he began, "Dad, there's something I need to tell you... about me and Yash."

His dad listened attentively, his expression a mix of curiosity and concern. As Sidharth poured his heart out, explaining his love for Yash and the support they had for each other, his dad's eyes softened with understanding.

"Sidhu, love knows no bounds," his dad interrupted gently, placing a hand on Sidharth's shoulder. "I support you both wholeheartedly. Yash has been a pillar of strength for you, and I can see the depth of your bond. You have my blessing."

Tears welled up in Sidharth's eyes, overwhelmed by his dad's acceptance and support. "Thank you, Dad," he whispered, his voice choked with emotion.

His dad pulled him into a tight embrace, pride and gratitude evident in his voice. "Do you realize, Sidhu, Yash went through hell, utterly shattered. He cared for you with a depth that words can't capture. I consider myself blessed to have him stand by you, my son."

Overwhelmed, Sidhu burst into tears and responded, “I know.”

In that heartfelt moment, the bond between father and son, and the impact of Yash's presence in their lives, resonated deeply, affirming the strength of their family's love and acceptance.

After leaving the room, Uncle Rohit remarked, “He told me about you both. I'm happy that you are his partner. Take good care of him and yourself, and never blame yourself for what happened. That's fate. We should thank God for giving him back.”

“Hmmm,” I replied, embracing him with tear-filled eyes.

“Cheer up, Yashi,” Uncle Rohit encouraged.

"Yes," I nodded with a smile, feeling the warmth of his support. Uncle Rohit departed after a few days, leaving behind a sense of reassurance and gratitude for the precious gift of Sidhu's recovery.

Together, we navigated the challenges, striving to reclaim a semblance of normalcy in our lives. Along this journey, we embraced the therapeutic power of Yoga, finding solace and strength in its practice. Additionally, we explored the harmonious fusion of Carnatic music and the soulful strains of the violin, creating a shared expression of resilience.

Embarking on the journey of creating our YouTube channel marked a significant moment for us. Through daily uploads, we shared a mosaic of our lives – from musical fusions to spontaneous dance moments and daring cooking experiments. Our channel became a canvas for expressing everything we wanted to share with our audience. It was a platform where our creativity and passions found a home, fostering a connection with viewers as they joined us on this exciting venture.

It wasn't a swift process, but after a year of unwavering dedication, Sidharth gradually regained his mental health. The journey demanded patience, understanding, and perseverance. Despite losing two semesters, the joy of his recovery overshadowed the setbacks. Looking forward with optimism, Sidharth prepared to resume his academic pursuits in the upcoming year, steadfastly pursuing his dreams alongside the unwavering support of our shared journey.

As the poignant chapters of our story unfolded through the recording, we decided to halt for the day. The weight of the emotional narrative lingered in the air, a testament to the shared struggles, resilience, and the profound journey we had undertaken together."

In that moment of pause, a sense of reflection and gratitude enveloped us, allowing the impact of our experiences to settle. The recording session became a poignant interlude, marking a chapter in our lives that, though challenging, carried the seeds of growth, strength, and the enduring bond that held us together."

CHAPTER XIX

"Unbreakable Bonds: Navigating Love, Family Expectations, and Unspoken Realities"

On the seventeenth recording day, Sidharth delivered a flawless voiceover, capturing the essence of the unfolding events with precision and emotion.

"Yash's phone buzzed, and with an air of casual ease, he answered his father's call, "Hey, Dad, what's going on?"

His dad took a deep breath before broaching the topic, "Yashi, your mother and I believe it's time for you to consider marriage. We're thinking of getting you engaged to Lena. What do you think?"

"Dad, I'm really not interested, and honestly, I don't have any feelings for her," Yashi responded firmly.

His dad persisted, "Yashi, consider it carefully. Lena is a good match for you."

Yashi responded with a firm tone, "Dad, I appreciate your concern, but I can't go along with this. I've already chosen my life partner, and it's Sidharth. No matter how much you pressure me, it won't change."

His dad, disapproving of the relationship, persisted in his persuasion. Despite the relentless efforts, Yashi remained resolute and unwavering in his decision.

As the conversation continued, Yashi emphasized, "Dad, I understand your reservations, but Sidharth and I share a genuine connection. I hope, with time, you'll come to accept our relationship."

Despite the tension, Yashi stood by his choice. The conversation reached an impasse, and his dad reluctantly concluded, "We'll talk about this later. By the way, Lena is coming to Thailand for one week."

The call ended with an air of unresolved tension, leaving Yashi to contemplate the challenging situation ahead.

Upon his dad's announcement, Lena arrived for a week-long visit. To accommodate her stay, we assigned the room I had previously used. With Yashi preoccupied with work commitments, the responsibility fell on me to accompany Lena during my free hours after classes despite her initial disagreement. It became apparent that, under the circumstances, this arrangement was the only viable option.

Yashi consistently disregarded Lena, his aversion stemming from childhood. Despite Lena's persistent efforts to create opportunities to be with Yashi, his disinterest remained evident. The longstanding dislike formed a barrier, making it challenging for Lena to establish a connection with Yashi.

Despite her attempts to establish a connection with Yashi, all efforts proved in vain. Throughout her brief stay, the unshakeable bond between Yashi and me became evident to her, leading her to realize that her envisioned engagement was nothing more than a dream. This realization prompted her to shorten her visit, leaving with a newfound understanding that Yashi's heart was already committed elsewhere.

Despite planning a week-long visit, she curtailed it after just four days, acknowledging the impracticality of her aspirations.

In those four days, an unspoken understanding prevailed – the proposed engagement was not a feasible reality. Lena departed with a clear perception of the unbreakable bond shared between Yashi and me.

As the day concludes, I'll bring our conversation to a close."

CHAPTER XX

"Dances of Destiny: Love's Choreography in the Tapestry of Time"

On recording day, Yash's voiceover resonated with a bittersweet truth.

"After Lena's departure, a plan blossomed to visit Bharath two weeks later. Sidharth's yearning for the comforting presence of his dad and grandparents infused the plan with a poignant undertone. For me, the anticipation held a unique beauty, as years of separation heightened the significance of the impending reunion, promising a tapestry of shared moments and the rekindling of long-missed connections.

During our trip to India, Sidharth and I got caught up in this tense drama with my parents. Despite my folks returning from abroad for a family visit, things went south when they insisted me to marry Lena, a notion I wasn't keen on. Sidharth's dad tried to mediate, but the tension lingered.

It's worth noting that Sidharth's dad had been cool with our relationship from the get-go. As if that weren't enough, my own parents jumped into the mix, escalating an already complicated situation. Sadly, even our grandparents were affected, expressing their disappointment. What was supposed to be a time for family connection turned into a tough, emotionally charged ordeal for all of us.

As the situation worsened, I recognized the need to take charge and make a decision.

"I am willing to comply with your wishes, but I need to have a conversation with Sidharth first," I firmly stated.

My dad, visibly angered, responded, "If only you had made this decision earlier, we could have avoided this entire situation."

"I apologize," I expressed, realizing the consequences of my delayed choice.

I approached Sidharth, witnessing the emotional toll the situation had taken on him. As soon as I entered, he rushed into my arms, seeking solace in a heartfelt hug. With tears in his eyes, we shared a moment of profound connection. I gently consoled him, reassuring him that we would face the challenges together. In the simplicity of that embrace, words became unnecessary, and our shared understanding spoke volumes.

Silence lingered as my parents resolved to expedite our wedding plans within a week. In the midst of this, I received a call from Lena, to whom I explained the circumstances. The news of the impending wedding brought a mix of emotions; Lena, Sidharth, his dad, our grandparents, Ankitha, and I found ourselves in a shared sense of unhappiness. Tensions ran high, casting a palpable strain over our relationships.

The grand wedding day was a splendid affair, adorned with vibrant flowers, elegant decorations, and joyful laughter. The ceremony unfolded in a picturesque venue, where family and friends gathered to witness the union of two hearts.

Lena was resplendent in a vibrant lehenga, a traditional Indian outfit. Her ensemble featured intricate golden embroidery on a rich burgundy fabric, with shimmering sequins that caught the light, accentuating the grace of her movements. The flowing skirt of her lehenga cascaded elegantly, reflecting the hues of a setting sun. Her blouse, in a matching burgundy hue, was adorned with delicate patterns, adding a touch of elegance to her ensemble. Completing her look was a sheer dupatta, draped gracefully over one shoulder, embellished with golden borders that added a regal flair to her attire.

Sidharth and Yash looked dashing in their North Indian attire. Sidharth wore a traditional sherwani in a deep royal blue, embellished with intricate silver embroidery that shimmered in the light. The rich fabric draped elegantly over his frame, accentuating his stature. Paired with a matching churidar, his ensemble exuded a sense of regal charm and sophistication. Yash, on the other hand, opted for a classic kurta-pajama set in a subtle shade of cream. His kurta featured intricate thread work in shades of gold and silver, adding a touch of elegance to his ensemble. The simplicity of his attire highlighted his charismatic personality, making him a striking presence amidst the festivities.

Before the wedding ceremony began, I stepped forward to address the audience, just as my parents were about to intervene.

“Ladies and gentlemen, thank you all for being here today on this special occasion.” I continued ..

“Before we proceed with the ceremony, I feel compelled to share a few words. In this moment, Lena and I stand here, not by our own choosing, but compelled by the insistence of our parents. Despite my heartfelt pleas and expressions of discomfort, our voices seem lost amidst the orchestrated arrangement of this union.”

“A wedding, a once-in-a-lifetime event, should be with the person you truly love. It’s with a heavy heart that we’ve decided to decline our own wedding, recognizing that our paths are not meant to intertwine as life partners."

"So, I'd like to take a moment to introduce the person who was meant to be my partner on this journey."

"Sidharth, please join me," I beckoned, and as he stepped onto the stage, he gently held my hands.

"Sidharth, the love of my life, has been more than a companion. He's illuminated unseen corners of my existence, casting a beam of light into my sorrowful life. In moments of darkness, he's been the comforting pillow, the attentive listener who understood me when my own parents failed to."

[I, grappling with overwhelming emotions, struggled to articulate my feelings. In a moment of solace, Sidharth offered comforting words, instilling me with the strength to share more. Grateful for Sidharth's support, I found the courage to continue expressing my emotions.]

"Words can't capture the depth of my gratitude for the wonderful moments he's given me, for holding me tightly during my toughest times and for moulding me into a new Yash that you see today."

[I chuckled, tightly holding Sidharth's hand, a silent bond that reflected the strength of our shared journey.]

"Thank you, Sidharth, for standing unwaveringly beside me. You are my eye-opener, and with you, I am a hundred percent happy."

[Turning to Sidharth, I continued with a warm smile.]

"Let's cherish the memories we've created together and continue supporting each other as we journey down different paths"..

[Turning to Lena, I expressed with heartfelt gratitude.]

Lena, your understanding and support during this challenging time are deeply appreciated. Without you, this would have been impossible.

Although our paths may be diverging, we want to express sincere gratitude to each of you for being a part of our lives.

[I turned to Sidharth, the air filled with a quiet anticipation. With genuine affection in my voice, I expressed]

"Sidharth, you are the heartbeat of my life, the melody to my moments. I long to spend the rest of my days wrapped in the warmth of our love. Will you make me the happiest person alive and marry me?"

"Yes, with all my heart, it's a hundred percent yes," Sidharth responded, his eyes reflecting the depth of his emotions.

[We exchanged wedding rings, a moment of profound significance that left everyone present in awe—except for those who were privy to the secret plan. With the unwavering support of Uncle Rohit, Ankitha, and Lena, their carefully orchestrated surprise unfolded seamlessly, casting a spell of enchantment over the gathering. The air was filled with joy and astonishment, marking the beginning of a beautiful chapter in our journey together.]

"Napoleon Hill once said: "It is strange but true that the most important turning points of life often come at the most unexpected times and in the most unexpected ways."

"Ours is an example."

"Thank you, everyone, for being here with us during this emotional chapter of our lives. Your presence and support mean the world to us as we navigate through this period of change and growth."

[I concluded.]

A brief hush enveloped the room before transforming into exuberant applause. Amid the joyful clamour, Ankita, our cousins, and Lena cheekily called for a kiss.

Succumbing to the playful request, I shared a beautiful kiss with Sidharth. In that enchanting moment, surrounded by laughter and support, we sealed a memory of love and unity.

Wrapping up the recording, he exhaled and concluded with a beautiful smile on his face."

CHAPTER XXI

"Serenading Truth: A Love Chronicle Defying Stereotypes."

On our twentieth recording day, Sidharth and I decided to share our story through my voice on our YouTube channel.

Dear World,

We are a BL couple, and we have chosen to share our journey with you for a special reason - to challenge the unfortunate perception that some people hold about gay and lesbian marriages. There is a misconception, a curse, attached to our love, and we want to change that narrative. If our story can open just one person's eyes, it will make us incredibly happy.

We are doing this because we believe that the people watching our videos should be open-minded. We want to challenge stereotypes and showcase that love knows no boundaries, no gender. It's a simple plea for understanding, acceptance, and empathy.

Everyone has the right to choose their life partner, and that's a right we hold dear. So, we are sharing our journey in the hope that it resonates with others who might be facing similar challenges. We want people to see beyond societal norms and prejudices and understand that love is love, no matter who it's between.

For us, the key to a successful relationship is harmony. It's not just about sharing a space; it's about understanding and complementing each other. Without that harmony, living together loses its purpose. We want to highlight the beauty of two individuals coming together in a symphony of love and understanding.

As you join us in this journey, know it's more than just our tale. It's a gentle plea to embrace love in its every guise, to tear down the walls of stereotype, and to let each soul shine true. In these shared moments, we seek to spin a tale of pure simplicity, of quiet beauty, and, above all, the freedom to love without masks. Remember, it's your actions, not just your words, that mold the world. Let our story be a whisper of change, inspiring others to embrace their truth.

To each viewer and subscriber, may your dreams soar as high as your favorite video, and may every click bring joy, inspiration, and endless positivity into your lives. Thank you for being a cherished part of our journey!

With immense satisfaction and joy, we concluded recording the chapters of our life journey to date.

CHAPTER XXII

"Silent Whispers: Yash's Last Day Confession"

"On the last recording day, Yash's secret revelations added a touch of beauty to our shared journey.

Sidharth, I apologize for not sharing this with you until now. There's something important I need to tell you.

In those days, my heart quietly discovered its affection for you. Unsure of your sentiments, I hesitated to speak. The dilemma of whether to share my feelings or keep them hidden created a gentle turmoil within. Fortunately, just when I needed clarity, a beautiful incident unfolded, weaving serendipity into our story.

During a weekend gathering with your friends in this cozy home, as the evening was drawing to a close and your friends were departing, I prepared to guide you to bed. It was then, under the soft glow of the lamp and the lingering warmth of our conversations, that you, emboldened by alcohol, confessed your love for me, surprising me with a tender kiss. Stunned momentarily, I couldn't help but burst into laughter at the unexpectedness of the moment. However, you, lost in the haze of intoxication, seemed to drift into a gentle slumber, your heart laid bare in that fleeting, beautiful instant.

The next morning, you appeared refreshed, behaving as if nothing had occurred. I chose to act as if the event didn't transpire, realizing you had no recollection of the night. It was in that moment of clarity that I understood the depth of your care and concern for me, unraveling the mystery behind your actions and solidifying our connection. Moreover, the joy of knowing you felt the same way added a beautiful simplicity to my heart's delight.

Since that day, my care and concern for you mirrored the same devotion you showed me. No matter your actions, I refrained from anger. Typically protective of my belongings, I made exceptions for you. You became the sole person I entrusted with the key to my heart, creating a unique and exceptional bond between us.

The day of the accident, everything crumbled beneath me, leaving me lost and struggling to find my way. It's a miracle I made it through, and I owe it all to Uncle Rohit's unwavering support.

I remember those days, the endless hours spent in waiting rooms, the sleepless nights filled with prayers and tears. Every moment felt like an eternity, every breath a silent plea for your recovery. But through it all, I held on to one truth, one unwavering belief—that our love, our bond, would be the anchor that would guide us through this storm.

And as we move forward, as we navigate the uncertainties of life together, I want you to know one thing—Sidharth, I can't even begin to imagine a life without you. Every moment, every breath, is precious beyond measure. Always stay by my side. My love for you runs deeper than words can express. Every syllable of my voice trembles with the pain of knowing how close I came to losing you. [Yash's voice racked with pain].

I don't know why I kept this from you until now, but at this moment, I feel compelled to express my feelings. Sidhu, I love you wholeheartedly. Thank you for being the radiant light in my life. You are, and always will be, mine – Only mine."

Yash concluded the recording with a poignant pause, letting the sentiments linger in the air.

“beyond Words: Navigating Life’s Narration”

Picture life as a beautiful story, where we hold the pen. This tale whispers that our choices, like plot twists, guide us through ups and downs, making our journey uniquely ours.

At its heart is a simple plea to choose joy, despite the noisy demands around us. It nudges us to be the captains of our ships, steering clear of pressures that could disrupt the harmony of our shared voyage.

Love, the storyteller insists, isn’t just skin-deep. It’s in the kindness of character and the grace of behaviour. This story paints love as a masterpiece, where the true beauty lies in the essence of a person rather than just their looks.

Woven into the narrative is a call to keep the romance alive. It’s a gentle reminder to sprinkle our days with the magic of passion, transforming routine into a captivating dance of moments that sparkle.

In our imperfect world, love blooms in acceptance and respect. As partners, we become guiding stars in moments of need, lighthouses in times of confusion. We embody the unwavering light in each other’s darkness, painting our shared canvas with the beauty of unconditional love. It’s a poetic dance echoing the story’s plea to choose joy, crafting a masterpiece of genuine connection and heartfelt simplicity.

Our lives are full of ups and downs. True love stands as a pillar in our lives of joy and pain, irrespective of gender. So let’s live and enjoy life to the fullest with our loved ones, making it more beautiful with each passing moment.

In these simple words, the story aims to capture the narrator’s voice, a friendly guide through the tale. It’s a canvas of authenticity, celebrating the pursuit of happiness, cherishing connections that withstand time. So, let's embrace the narrator's voice, a companion in this journey, urging us to paint our lives with the colours of joy, love, and genuine connections.

---------------------------- -------------------------

www.ingramcontent.com/pod-product-compliance
Lightning Source LLC
La Vergne TN
LVHW091224150826
845673LV00003B/1002